The Jam Panda
Blue Story Book

JAM PANDAS

The Jam Panda

Blue Story Book

Written by Caroline Repchuk
Illustrated by Stephanie Boey

P
PARRAGON

A PARRAGON BOOK

Published by Parragon
13 Whiteladies Road, Clifton, Bristol BS8 1PB

Produced by The Templar Company plc,
Pippbrook Mill, London Road, Dorking, Surrey RH4 1JE

Designed by Janie Louise Hunt

Printed in Italy

ISBN 0 75252 606 5

Contents

The Jam Panda Picnic

Big Bamboo's Blackcurrant Birthday

Grandma's Strawberry Surprise

GRANDMA

MA AND PA JAM

BIG BAMBOO

JIM JAM

PEACHES AND PLUM

THE
Jam Panda Picnic

Peaches and Plum were excited!
Today was the day the Jam Pandas had their picnic.

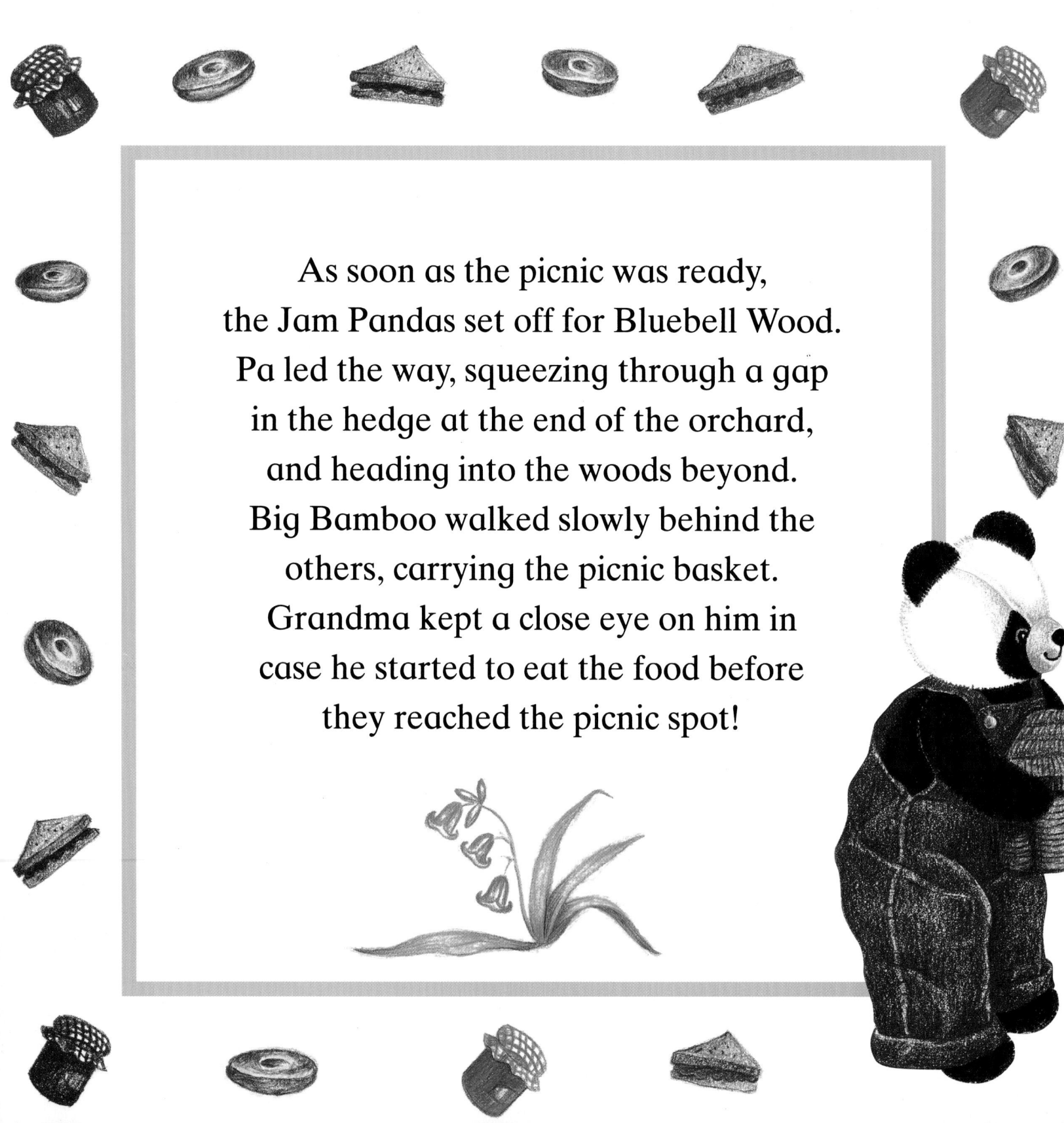

As soon as the picnic was ready,
the Jam Pandas set off for Bluebell Wood.
Pa led the way, squeezing through a gap
in the hedge at the end of the orchard,
and heading into the woods beyond.
Big Bamboo walked slowly behind the
others, carrying the picnic basket.
Grandma kept a close eye on him in
case he started to eat the food before
they reached the picnic spot!

Before long the Jam Pandas came to a clearing, where they stopped and spread out their blanket. Springtime was the very best time of the year in Bluebell Wood, with bluebells covering the ground in a thick carpet of blue. "Take care not to tread on the flowers!" said Pa.

As it was too early for lunch, Peaches and Plum decided to go and play hide and seek. "Come on Big Bamboo!" shouted Peaches. But Big Bamboo was almost asleep already. "Umph!" he said. "Wake me up when it's time for lunch."

The Jam Panda twins ran into the wood. They stopped by a big tree, and started their game. Plum covered his eyes and started counting up to twenty while Peaches ran off to hide.

Peaches soon found a good hiding place
in a big, twisted old oak tree which was
hollow inside. It was perfect!
From her hiding place she could
hear Plum, who was still counting.
"...eighteen, nineteen, twenty. I'm coming!"
he called.

Peaches didn't think it would take
Plum long to find her. She waited and waited.
But Plum didn't come. After a while, she
called out, "Plum, I'm here!"
But Plum still didn't come.

Peaches decided that she had waited long
enough. She didn't want to miss lunch!
She crawled out of her hiding place
and set off back to the picnic.

But poor Peaches couldn't fine her way back! She walked on and on through Bluebell Wood. "Ma!" she cried. "Pa! Grandma!" But nobody answered. Peaches was well and truly lost. She sat down on a tree stump and started to cry.

Meanwhile, Plum had been searching high and low for Peaches but he just couldn't find her. He started to get really worried, and after looking everywhere he could think of, he returned to the other pandas and told them that Peaches had gone missing.

"Don't worry, Plum," said Grandma,
who had been unpacking the picnic.
"We will *all* look for Peaches!"

The Jam Pandas searched all through the wood, but there was no sign of Peaches. Just then, as Ma was getting really worried, she spotted a trail of broken bluebells, leading into the wood. "Jumping Jamspoons!" said Pa. "Peaches must have forgotten not to tread on the bluebells. We can follow her trail!"

In no time at all, the trail led the Jam Pandas to Peaches. She was curled up fast asleep under a beech tree. Plum woke her up with a big hug. They were very glad to see each other!

Just then, Big Bamboo's tummy rumbled and everyone laughed. "I think it's picnic time," said Grandma.

Back at the picnic spot they were all soon tucking into a delicious jammy feast. Big Bamboo insisted he needed an extra large helping of blackcurrant jam to restore his energy levels after the search, and Ma made sure Peaches got a specially big helping of her favourite peach jam. "At least one thing is certain," chuckled Pa, biting into a big jammy doughnut. "When it comes to picnics, Grandma always makes sure *nothing* is missing!"

BIG BAMBOO'S
Blackcurrant Birthday

Big bamboo was such a lazy panda.
He always woke up late.
One morning he woke up very late indeed.
As he lay dozing he thought he heard a
noise coming from downstairs.
What was all that banging and clattering?
"Oh, no!" said Big Bamboo. "Work!"

Big Bamboo didn't like work at all. He much preferred eating. He climbed out of bed and got dressed. Then he crept downstairs on tiptoes, (*which for a big panda like him was not easy!*), and sneaked out of the house.

He was going to find somewhere to hide
so he wouldn't have to work!

He didn't realise the other Jam Pandas had heard him.
They were looking at each other, smiling.

Little did Big Bamboo know that
the 'work' was all for him!
He wasn't very good at remembering
things, (*unless, of course, it was where his
secret jam supply was hidden!*) and had
forgotten that today was his birthday.
But the other Jam Pandas had remembered,
and now they were secretly preparing a
special birthday party just for him.

They worked hard all morning, and at last everything was ready.

The cottage had been decorated with balloons, and the table was covered with jam sandwiches, jam sponges and even jam jelly!

There were party hats and a lot of presents.

Grandma Jam knew what Big Bamboo's favourite present would be – a specially big pot of delicious blackcurrant jam!

All they needed now was Big Bamboo and the party could begin. But where was he? The Jam Pandas set out to look for him. First they looked in the garden.

"He can't be far away," said Ma Jam.

Peaches and Plum, the cheeky twins, searched
for Big Bamboo in the orchard.
"I'm sure they'll find him there," said Ma Jam.

But he wasn't in the orchard.
"Perhaps he's in the wood," said Pa.

Pa searched all through the wood but
Big Bamboo wasn't there either.
Just then little Jim Jam, the
baby panda, began crawling away.
"Big Bam! Big Bam!" he said.
"Jumping Jamspoons!" said Grandma.
"That little chap's got an idea!"

Jim Jam was heading straight for the blackcurrant patch.
In no time at all he had disappeared
amongst the bushes.

Peaches and Plum were not far behind him.
"Look!" they shouted, pointing
excitedly at the blackcurrant patch.
"It's Big Bamboo!"

Big Bamboo loved blackcurrants.
They were his very favourite fruit of all.
He had been hiding there all morning
and he had eaten nearly every blackcurrant
in the patch! Now he looked like
a very poorly panda indeed.
"Ooooh!" he groaned.
"My tummy hurts!"

Back at the cottage, Big Bamboo
went straight to bed.
"Ooooh!" he groaned again.
"What a birthday!"
Grandma set to work at once and prepared
a pot of her special medicinal jam.
Before long Big Bamboo was feeling much
better, but he was very disappointed
that he had missed his party, and
spoiled his big surprise.
"I'm very sorry," he told the others.
"I'll try not to be so greedy in future."

The next day he got up, went downstairs and... Surprise!

HAPPY BIRTHDAY BIG BAMBOO!

The Jam Pandas had decided that Big Bamboo had suffered enough for his greediness, and to hold the party a day late. Besides, it would be terrible to waste all those lovely jam sandwiches!

GRANDMA'S
Strawberry Surprise

Grandma was very proud
of the delicious jams she made.

All of the Jam Pandas had their own favourite
flavour of jam. Grandma's was strawberry. There
was nothing she liked more than having a nice cup
of strawberry tea, with a strawberry jam sandwich.

But one day, when Grandma went to fetch some strawberry jam from the cupboard for tea, she got quite a shock. It was all gone — Big Bamboo had polished off the last jar as a midnight feast!

"Oh well," said Grandma. "I shall just have to make some more."

But the strawberries had not been growing well that year. Grandma looked anxiously at the patch of little strawberries in the garden. They didn't look big enough to make jam with.

Just then Grandma had an idea.

In the kitchen, Grandma got out her
special book. It was very old. It had been
given to her by her Great-Grandma.
It might even have belonged to
her Great-Great-Grandma.

She searched through the dusty pages
until she found what she was looking for.
It was a recipe for a magic growing potion.
Grandma decided to make some to put on
the little strawberries in the garden.

Soon Grandma was busy
preparing the magic potion.

She was so busy that she didn't
notice that Big Bamboo had eaten
one of the secret ingredients while
she wasn't looking.

When the potion was ready
Grandma put it in a watering can
and went outside.

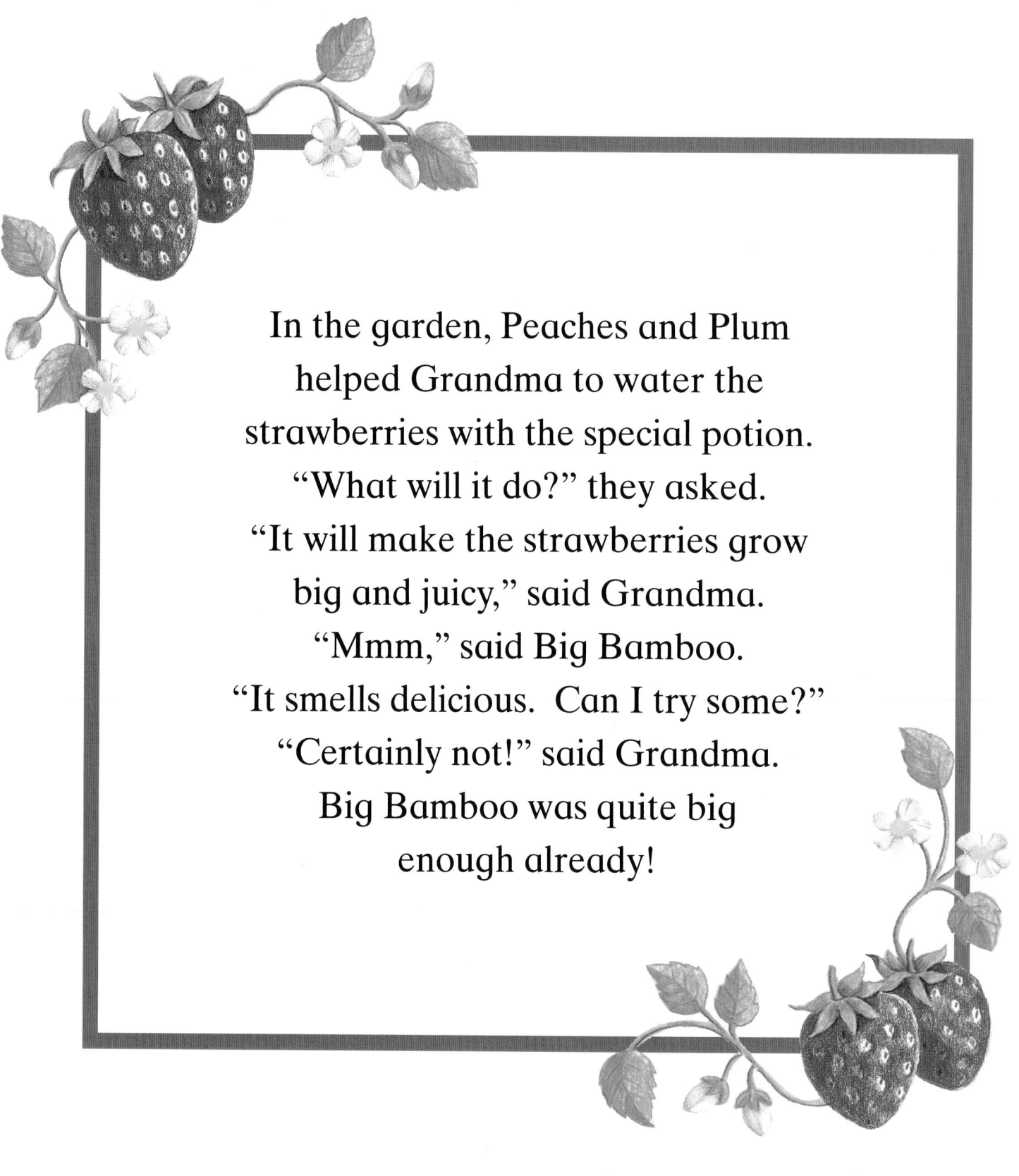

In the garden, Peaches and Plum
helped Grandma to water the
strawberries with the special potion.
"What will it do?" they asked.
"It will make the strawberries grow
big and juicy," said Grandma.
"Mmm," said Big Bamboo.
"It smells delicious. Can I try some?"
"Certainly not!" said Grandma.
Big Bamboo was quite big
enough already!

Nothing happened to the strawberries
all that day. Peaches and Plum kept going
to look at them just in case.

But that night something
very strange happened.
The strawberries started to grow.

And grow!

When Grandma went into the garden the next day the strawberries were bigger than wheelbarrows!

"Jumping Jamspoons!" she said. "That wasn't supposed to happen! I must have forgotten something."

Big Bamboo blushed as he realised he had eaten the missing ingredient.

Grandma couldn't pick the enormous strawberries to make them into jam. She couldn't even lift them! Neither could Ma or the twins. Not even Pa and Big Bamboo could lift them, though they tried and tried. Poor Grandma didn't know what to do. She couldn't bear to waste all those lovely strawberries.

Then she had another idea.

She told Peaches and Plum that she had a special errand for them to do.

The next day Peaches and Plum visited all the Jam Pandas' friends to invite them to a Spring Strawberry Feast that afternoon, in the garden of Tumbledown Cottage.

And Pa went to the farm to get
a whole wheelbarrowful of cream!

All of their friends came to the feast.

Everyone agreed it was the scrummiest Spring Strawberry Feast they had ever been to.

"These strawberries are delicious," chuckled Grandma. "But I think I'll leave nature to do the growing next time!"

Big Bamboo didn't say anything.

He was busy eating strawberries and cream, and wondering whether there was any magic potion left that he could use on his blackcurrants!

• THE END •